Sofia the First

The Royal Games

Written by Catherine Hapka

Based on an episode by Laurie Israel and Rachel Ruderman

Illustrated by Character Building Studio and the Disney Storybook Artists

DISNEP PRESS

New York • Los Angeles

SUSTAINABLE FORESTRY INITIATIVE

Certified Chain of Custody
Promoting Sustainable Forestry

www.sfiprogram.org
SFI-01415

The SFI label applies to the text stock

One beautiful day in Enchancia, three grand coaches coast to a landing at the royal picnic grounds. The herald announces the arrival of three royal families from three different kingdoms: Wei-Ling, Khaldoun, and Enchancia.

"The tri-kingdom picnic is no ordinary picnic," Amber tells Sofia as they climb out of their family's coach.

Sofia looks around at all the people, the fancy tent, and a buffet table piled high with delicious food. "I'm starting to see that!"

Sofia greets the princesses from the other families. Princess Jun of Wei-Ling is sweet and silly. Princess Maya of Khaldoun has a friendly grin and a sporty look. Sofia can't wait to get to know them better.

"Sofia!" James exclaims, running over. "You've got to see this."
He leads her to a huge trophy—the Golden Chalice.

"All the kids at the picnic play games, and the kingdom that wins the most games gets to keep the chalice until the next picnic," James says. "I've always wanted to win it!"

James explains that Amber doesn't like playing the games. He's hoping that Sofia can take Amber's place this year.

"Teammates?" James sticks out his hand.

Sofia smiles. "Teammates!"

Sofia and James change their clothes. Then Sofia meets Maya's brother, Prince Khalid, and Jun's brother, Prince Jin.

Baileywick calls for the first game to start —Flying Horseshoe Toss.

At first Sofia doesn't understand why it's called Flying Horseshoe Toss. Then she sees the wings on the horseshoes! That makes the game extra tricky, since the horseshoes like to swoop off course. Jin goes first, and his horseshoe lands nowhere near the stake. "Good try, Jin!" Maya says.

Jun's horseshoe lands on the buffet table. "Oops!" She giggles. "Someone tell my horseshoe it's not time for lunch."

Then it's James's turn. His horseshoe lands near the stake. "Best throw so far!" Jin says.

Princess Maya goes next. Her horseshoe lands even closer to the stake than James's!

"Nice one," Khalid says.

"Sofia, it's up to you," James says. "If you get closer than Maya, we win."

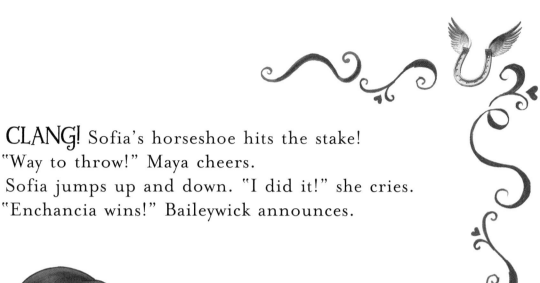

CLANG! Sofia's horseshoe hits the stake!
"Way to throw!" Maya cheers.
Sofia jumps up and down. "I did it!" she cries.
"Enchancia wins!" Baileywick announces.

"We won!" James exclaims. "I've never won before!"

"Nicely done, Sofia," Jin says.

James points at the others. "We're the best!" he shouts.
"Enchancia's going to win this year!"

"All right, we heard you," Jin says.

James ignores him. "Come on, Sofia. Let's go win the next game!" he cries, rushing off.

Sofia is surprised by the way James is acting. "He's just really excited," she tells the others with a sheepish smile.

Maya frowns. "I guess so."

Baileywick calls, "Time for the Golden Egg on a Silver Spoon race."
Sofia balances her golden egg carefully. When Baileywick says, "Go,"
she races onto the course.

SPLAT! SPLAT! Jun and Khalid drop their eggs within moments.
Maya stumbles and almost loses hers but catches it just in time!
"Nice save," Sofia tells her.

"Sofia!" James says. "This is a race. There's no time to talk!"
That distracts Sofia. SPLAT!

James and Maya keep going. James almost wins, but at the last
second Maya passes him.

Everyone congratulates Maya—everyone except James, that is.
SPLAT! He throws his egg to the ground. "I would have won except the sun was in my eyes!" he complains.

"What a sore loser," Maya whispers to Jun.

Sofia hears her. "Sorry again," she says. "I'll go talk to James."

Sofia finds James getting ready for the next game. "Could you be a little nicer to the other kids?" she suggests.

"I'm not doing anything wrong," James insists. "I'm just trying to win."

"But, James..." Sofia begins.

It's no use. James is already rushing off.

The next game is Tri-Kingdom Triplenet.

James plays hard, doing everything he can to keep the ball from touching the ground on Enchancia's side of the triangle. In the end, James and Sofia are the winners.

"We won and you lost!" he jeers at the other teams afterward.

Sofia tries to stop James from taunting them. But he won't listen.
"We don't want to play anymore," Maya says at last.
"We don't, either," Jin agrees. "If you want the chalice so badly, you can have it. We quit."
"Sorry, Sofia," Jun adds.

James shrugs. "I don't get it. Why is everyone quitting?" he asks Sofia.

"Because they're not having any fun," Sofia says. "You've been a bad sport all day. I don't want to be your teammate anymore."

"Sofia!" James exclaims, sounding upset. "Come back!"

As Sofia hurries away, she notices the adults playing a game nearby.
They're all laughing and having fun. None of them seem to care
who is winning.

That gives Sofia an idea. . . .

"There's something you need to see," Sofia tells James.
She drags him over to watch the adults play Bewitching
Bowling. James sees his dad mess up his turn—and laugh.
"Oh, well," King Roland says. "Better luck next time—I hope!"

"See?" Sofia says to James. "Games are supposed to be fun—whether
you win or lose."
"I guess I haven't been much fun to play with," says James.

James finds the other kids and apologizes for being a sore loser—and a sore winner.

"I forgot that the tri-kingdom picnic is all about getting together and having a good time. I'm really sorry."

The kids decide to forgive James, and the games continue.

At the end of the day, Khaldoun wins the Golden Chalice.
And Sofia is happy to see that nobody cheers louder than James.
"Maybe next year we'll win," she tells him. "Teammates?"
He grins and shakes her hand. "Teammates!"